HANS CHRISTIAN ANDERSEN & ALAN MARKS
**THE UGLY DUCKLING**

Hans Christian Andersen

# THE UGLY DUCKLING

*illustrated by Alan Marks · translated by Anthea Bell*

PICTURE BOOK STUDIO

It was summer, and the countryside looked beautiful. The wheat was golden, the oats were green, there were haystacks standing in the meadows, and the stork marched about on his long, red legs, chattering in Egyptian, a language his mother had taught him. The fields and meadows were surrounded by the great forest, and in the middle of the forest lay deep lakes. Yes, it was really beautiful out in the country.

An old manor house stood in the sunlight, with a deep moat around it. Huge burdock leaves grew all the way from the walls right down to the water, leaves so big that a child could stand upright under the largest of them as if in a thick, wild wood. A duck had made her nest here, and now she had to hatch her eggs, though she was getting tired of sitting on them. It took so long, and she hardly ever had any visitors. The other ducks would rather swim in the moat than sit under a burdock leaf and talk to her.

At last one of the eggs cracked, and then another. "Cheep, cheep!" said the live ducklings who had grown inside the shells, and were now sticking their heads out.

"Quack, quack!" said the mother duck, and they eagerly looked around them under the green leaves. Their mother let them stare as long as they liked. Green is good for the eyes.

"Oh, how big the world is!" said all the little ducklings. They had much more room to move about now than when they were still in the shell.

"You don't think this is the whole world, do you?" said their mother. "My goodness, the world's much bigger! It goes on beyond the garden, all the way into Parson's field, though I can't say I've been that far myself. Well, I suppose you've all arrived now." And she stood up. "Oh no, you haven't. The biggest egg's still there. How much longer is it going to take? I'm tired of hatching eggs!" she said, sitting down on it again.

"How are you doing, dear?" asked an old duck who had come calling.

"This last egg is taking forever!" said the duck. "It just won't hatch. But do look at the others! The sweetest little ducklings I ever saw, the image of that scoundrel their father who never comes to see me!"

"Let's see the egg that won't hatch," said the old duck. "It'll be a turkey's egg, you mark my words. I was fooled that way once myself, and oh, the trouble I had with those chicks! Turkeys are scared of the water, you see! I simply couldn't get them to go in. I quacked at them and I snapped at them, but it was no use. Where's the egg, then? Yes, that's a turkey's egg for sure. You'd better leave it alone and teach the other little ones to swim."

"I'll sit on it a bit longer," said the duck. "I've been hatching it so long already, I can wait until the harvest's in."

"Please yourself," said the old duck, and she went away.

At last the big egg hatched. "Cheep, cheep!" said the duckling, tumbling out. He was very big and very ugly. The duck looked at him.

"What a huge big duckling he is!" she said. "None of the others look like that! Maybe he's a turkey chick after all? Oh, well, we'll soon find out. He's going into the water if I have to push him in myself!"

Next day the weather was beautiful, with the sun shining down on all the green burdock leaves. The mother duck took her whole family down to the moat. Splash! Into the water she went. "Quack, quack!" she said, and the ducklings tumbled in too, one by one. They went right under the water and came up again at once, swimming beautifully. Their legs knew just what to do. Even the ugly grey duckling could swim.

"Well, he's not a turkey after all," said the mother duck. "See how well he moves his legs and how upright he is! He's my own little duckling, and quite attractive if you look closely. Quack, quack! Come along now, I'm going to take you out into the world and introduce you to everyone in the poultry yard. Mind you keep close to me, so you don't get trodden on, and watch out for the cat!"

So off they went to the poultry yard, where there was a terrible noise going on. Two families were fighting over an eel's head. In the end the cat got it.

"That's the way of the world, see?" said the mother duck, and she licked her bill. She would have liked that eel's head herself. "Come along now, hurry up, and bow to the old duck over there. She's the best bred fowl in this yard; she has Spanish blood, that's why she's so fat, and as you can see, she wears a red rag around her leg. That's something special, the greatest mark of distinction a duck can have. It means she'll never have her neck wrung, and everyone, both man and beast, shows her great respect. Hurry up, and don't turn your toes in! A well brought up duckling keeps its legs wide apart, like its father and mother. Right, now bow your heads and say 'Quack!'"

So they did, but the other ducks in the yard stared at them and said, quacking noisily, "Look at all those ducklings! I suppose we're stuck with the whole lot of them now – as if there weren't enough of us already! My word, how ugly that one is! We certainly don't want him!" And one of the ducks flew at the ugly duckling and bit his neck.

"Leave that duckling alone!" said the other duck. "He never did you any harm!"

"Maybe not, but he's too big and he looks peculiar, so it serves him right!" said the duck that had bitten him.

"You have a fine brood there, Mother Duck," said the old duck with the red rag around her leg. "Very pretty, all of them, except that big one. He hasn't turned out well. You ought to hatch him out over again!"

"I can't do that, I'm afraid, Your Grace," said the mother duck. "I know he's no beauty, but he has a nice nature and he swims just as well as the others, maybe better. I think he may improve as he grows up, and he might not be so much bigger than the others then. He was in the egg too long, that's why he isn't quite the right shape." And she gently pecked his neck and smoothed his fluffy down. "Anyway, he's a drake," she added, "so his looks don't matter so much. I'm sure he's good and strong. He'll do!"

"Oh, well, the other ducklings are charming," said the old duck. "Make yourselves at home, and if you happen to find an eel's head lying around you can bring it to me."

So the ducklings settled in. But the poor duckling who had hatched out last and looked so ugly was pecked and shoved and mobbed by all the other ducks and hens. "He's too big!" they said. As for the turkey, who thought himself an Emperor because he had been born with spurs on, he puffed himself up like a ship in full sail and stalked over to the duckling, gobbling until he was bright red in the face. The poor little duckling didn't know what to do, and he felt very unhappy. He wished he wasn't so ugly, and the laughing stock of the whole poultry yard.

Well, that was the first day, and things went from bad to worse. Everyone chased the poor little duckling, including his own brothers and sisters, who were very nasty to him and kept saying, "You ugly duckling, I hope the cat gets you!" Even his mother said, "Dear me, I wish you weren't around!" The ducks snapped at him, the hens pecked him, and the girl who came to feed the poultry kicked him.

In the end he ran away. He flew over the hedge, scaring the little birds in the bushes up into the air themselves. "It's because I'm so ugly," thought the little duckling, shutting his eyes, but he went on running.

So he came to the great marsh where the wild ducks lived. He spent the night there, feeling very sad and tired.

Next morning the wild ducks flew up and saw the newcomer. "What sort of a bird are you?" they asked. The little duckling turned from one to another of them, being as polite as he could.

"My word, you're so ugly!" said the wild ducks. "Well, never mind that, so long as you don't want to marry into our family!"

The poor duckling had never thought of doing any such thing. All he wanted was to be allowed to stay there in the reeds, drinking a little water from the marsh. So he stayed for two days. Then two wild geese, or rather ganders, came along. They hadn't been hatched very long, and they would say anything.

"Listen, friend!" they told the duckling. "You're so ugly, we really like you! Want to come along and be one of us? There's another marsh not far off, with some sweet, pretty wild geese living in it, all of them girls with beautiful honking voices, and as you're so ugly you might as well try your luck with them."

Suddenly there was a loud "Bang! Bang!" overhead. Both wild geese fell into the reeds, dead, and the water ran red with their blood. The noise came again – "Bang! Bang!" Whole flocks of wild geese flew up from the reeds as the guns were fired once more. A great wild bird shoot was going on. There were hunters all around the marsh, some of them even up in the trees with their branches reaching out far over the reeds. Clouds of blue smoke drifted through the dark trees and hung above the water. Dogs came splashing through the mud; the reeds and rushes swayed from side to side. It was terrifying for the poor little duckling. He was bending his head to tuck it under his wing when he saw a huge great dog standing there, its tongue hanging out and its eyes gleaming ferociously. The dog bared its sharp teeth at the duckling – and then, splash! It went away again without touching him.

"Oh, thank goodness!" gasped the duckling. "I'm so ugly that even the dog doesn't want me!" And he lay there quite still while shot after shot rang out, and the pellets whistled through the reeds.

Not until late in the day did silence fall again, and even then the poor little duckling dared not move. He waited several hours before venturing to look around, and then he ran away from the marsh as far as he could go, over fields and meadows, in such a strong wind that he had a hard time getting anywhere.

In the evening he came to a poor little cottage. It was such a wretched place that it couldn't make up its mind which way to fall, so it stayed standing. The wind was blowing so hard that the duckling had to steady himself on his tail to keep his balance, and it blew harder and harder. Then he noticed that the door of the cottage was hanging off one hinge at such an angle that he could get through the crack and inside the room. So he did.

An old woman lived in this cottage, with her cat and her hen. The cat, whose name was Sonny, could arch his back and purr, and if you stroked him the wrong way his fur gave off sparks. The hen had very short legs, so the old woman called her Chickie Little-legs. She was good at laying eggs, and the old woman loved her like a child.

First thing next morning, the cat and the hen noticed the newcomer. The cat began to purr, and the hen began to cluck.

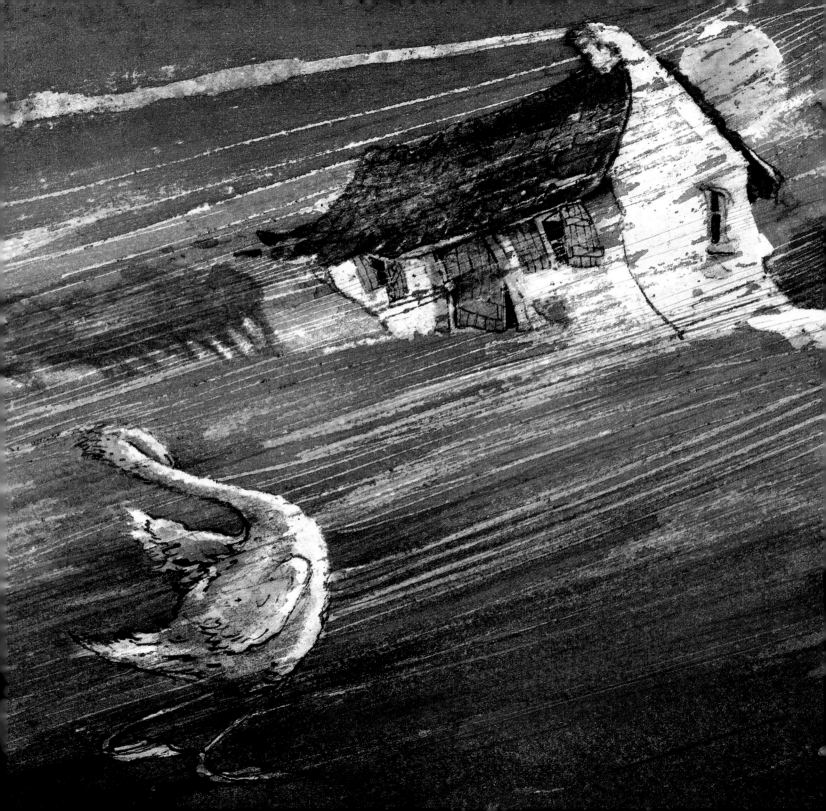

"What is it?" asked the old woman, looking around, but she had such poor eyesight that she thought the duckling was a fully grown fat duck which had lost its way. "Why, here's a good catch!" she said. "Now I can have duck's eggs, unless it's a drake! We'll soon find out!"

So the duckling was given a home for three weeks, on trial, but he laid no eggs. The cat was the master of the house, the hen was the lady of the house, and they always used to say, "We and the world!", because they thought they were half the world, and the better half of it too. The duckling wasn't so sure about that, but the hen dismissed his opinion.

"Can you lay eggs?" she inquired.

"No."

"Then hold your tongue!"

"Can you arch your back?" asked the cat. "Can you purr and give off sparks?"

"No."

"Then you've no right to offer an opinion when sensible folk are talking!"

So the duckling sat in a corner, feeling sad. Then he remembered the fresh air and the sunshine, and he longed to swim in the water so much that at last he had to tell the hen.

"What on earth is the matter with you?" she asked. "You have nothing to do, that's your trouble, or you wouldn't think of such things! Why not lay an egg, or purr? Then you'll feel better."

"But it's so lovely, swimming in the water!" said the duckling. "It's wonderful to put your head under and dive right down to the bottom!"

"Delightful, I'm sure!" said the hen. "You must be out of your mind! Don't just take my word for it, you ask the cat, the cleverest creature I know, whether he fancies swimming and diving! Or our mistress the old woman herself – and she's the wisest person in the world! Do you think she likes swimming and diving under water?"

"You don't understand," said the duckling.

"Well, if we don't understand, I can't think who would! Are you saying you know better than the cat or the old woman, not to mention me? Stop showing off, and give thanks for your luck! Here you are in a nice warm room, mixing with intelligent folk who can teach you things, and all you do is talk nonsense. It's not funny, I can tell you! I'm only saying so for your own good – your real friends are the people who tell you the truth, however unpleasent! Get on with it and lay some eggs, or learn to purr and give off sparks."

"I think I want to go out into the world," said the duckling.

"Who's stopping you?" said the hen.

So the duckling went off again. He swam in the water, and went diving down to the bottom, but he was so ugly that all the other creatures kept out of his way.

Summer was over; the leaves turned brown and yellow, the wind caught them, making them whirl and dance, and the air grew cold. The clouds were heavy with hail and snow, and a raven perched on the fence cawing with cold. It made you freeze to think of it. The poor little duckling was in a bad way.

One evening, as the sun was setting in a glorious sky, a whole flock of big and beautiful birds came out of the reeds. The duckling had never seen anything so lovely before. Their feathers were gleaming white, and they had long, graceful necks. They were swans. They uttered a strange cry, spread their magnificent wings, and flew away from that cold countryside to warmer lands where the water did not freeze. High, high in the air they rose, and the ugly little duckling felt very odd. He swam round and round in the water like a wheel, craning his neck to watch them go, and making such strange sounds himself that they quite frightened him. How could he ever forget those beautiful, happy birds?

When they were out of sight, he went diving down to the bottom, and by the time he came up he felt odder than ever. He did not know what the birds were called, or where they were going, but he loved them more than he had ever loved anything in his life. He was not envious – how could he even wish to be so beautiful himself? Poor, ugly little duckling, he would have been happy enough if the ordinary ducks would have let him stay in their yard.

It was a cold, cold winter. The duckling had to swim round and round to stop the water from freezing right over, but the hole he was keeping open grew smaller and smaller night by night. There was such a hard frost that the ice creaked, and the duckling had to move his legs all the time to keep his last little bit of water clear. Finally he was so tired that he gave up, and froze fast in the ice.

Early next morning a farmer came by, saw the duckling, went and broke the ice with his wooden clogs, and took the bird home to his wife, who revived him.

The farmer's children wanted to play with him, but the duckling thought they were going to hurt him, and he was so scared that he flew into the milk pail, splashing milk all over the room. The farmer's wife screeched and clapped her hands. Then he flew into the butter tub, and then into the flour barrel, and out again. Oh, what a mess he was! The woman screeched again and lashed out with a pair of tongs, and the children ran after the duckling, laughing and shouting and falling over each other as they tried to catch him. Luckily the door was open. The duckling flapped his way out into the bushes and the newly fallen snow, where he lay quite still.

Well, this story would be too sad if I told you all the duckling had to suffer that bitter winter. But when there was some warmth in the sun again, he was back among the reeds of the marsh. The larks were singing, and it was lovely spring weather.

Then the duckling spread his wings to fly. They were stronger than they used to be, and carried him powerfully away. Before he knew it, he was in a big garden, where there were apple trees in blossom, and fragrant lilac on long green branches above the waters of a winding stream. How beautiful and fresh it all was! Then three lovely white swans came swimming out of the undergrowth ahead of him. Their feathers ruffled as they glided over the water. The duckling recognized these beautiful birds, and a strange, sad feeling came over him again.

"I'll fly over to those royal birds, he thought. "They will hack me to death for coming near them, when I'm so ugly, but I don't mind! I'd rather be killed by them than pecked by the ducks and hens and kicked by the girl who looks after the poultry yard, and then suffer all winter!"

So he came down on the water and swam in the direction of the beautiful swans. Seeing him, they ruffled their feathers again and came swimming fast to meet him.

"Kill me," said the poor bird, bending his head low to the water and waiting for death to come. But what did he see there in the clear water? He saw his own reflection, and he was no longer a clumsy, grey, ugly bird – he was a swan himself.

It makes no difference where you are born, even in a poultry yard, if you have hatched out of a swan's egg!

Now he was glad of all he had suffered, since he could enjoy his good fortune and the beauty around him better for it. The great swans swam up, surrounding him and caressing him with their beaks.

Some children came into the garden to throw bread and grain to the birds. "Oh, look, there's a new swan!" cried the youngest child. "Yes, there's a new swan!" shouted the other children happily. They clapped their hands and danced about, and then ran to fetch their father and mother.

They threw bread and cake into the water, and they all said, "That new swan is the most beautiful of all! So young and handsome!" And the old swans bowed to him.

He felt very shy, and hid his head under his wing in embarrassment. It was almost too good to be true, but he wasn't proud, for a good heart is never proud.

He remembered how he had once been mocked and despised, and now he heard everyone saying he was the most beautiful of all those lovely birds. The lilac branches hung low above the water, and the sun shone warm and bright. He ruffled his feathers, raised his slender neck, and his heart was full of joy.

"I never dreamed of such happiness," he thought, "when I was the Ugly Duckling!"

A Michael Neugebauer Book
Copyright © 1989 Neugebauer Press, Salzburg, Austria
Original title: "Grimme Aelling"
Published and distributed in USA by Picture Book Studio, Saxonville, MA.
Distributed in Canada by Vanwell Publishing, St. Catharines, Ont.
Published in UK by Picture Book Studio, Neugebauer Press Ltd., London.
Distributed in UK by Ragged Bears, Andover.
Distributed in Australia by ERA Publications, Adelaide.
All rights reserved.
Printed in Belgium by Proost.

LIBRARY OF CONGRESS CATALOGING IN PUBLICATION DATA
Andersen, H.C. (Hans Christian), 1805-1875.
The ugly duckling/Hans Christian Andersen; illustrated by Alan Marks;
translated by Anthea Bell.
Translation of Grimme aelling.
Summary: An ugly duckling spends an unhappy year ostracized by the
other animals before he grows into a beautiful swan.
ISBN 0-88708-116-9
[1. Fairy tales.] I. Marks, Alan, 1957- ill. II. Bell, Anthea. III. Title.
PZ8.A542Ug 1989
[Fic]–dc19                          89-3975

Ask your bookseller for these other PICTURE BOOK STUDIO books
illustrated by Alan Marks:
NOWHERE TO BE FOUND by Alan Marks
THE FISHERMAN AND HIS WIFE by the Brothers Grimm